# Flapjacks from Paul Bunyan's Kitchen

Retold by Laura Appleton-Smith

Illustrated by Preston Neel

**Laura Appleton-Smith** holds a degree in English from Middlebury College.
Laura is a primary school teacher who has combined her talents in creative writing with
her experience in early childhood education to create *Books to Remember*.
She lives in New Hampshire with her husband, Terry.

**Preston Neel** was born in Macon, Georgia. Greatly inspired by Dr. Seuss,
he decided to become an artist at the age of four. Preston's advanced art studies took place at
the Academy of Art College San Francisco. Now Preston pursues his career in art with the hope of being
an inspiration himself, particularly to children who want to explore their endless bounds.

A Book to Remember™
Published by Flyleaf Publishing

For orders or information, contact us at **(800) 449-7006**.
Please visit our website at **www.flyleafpublishing.com**

Seventh Edition 5/19
Library of Congress Catalog Card Number: 2012939860
ISBN-13: 978-1-60541-147-7
Printed and bound in the USA at Worzalla Publishing, Stevens Point, WI

This story is based on several Paul Bunyan tall tales,
including one wonderful version collected and retold by S. E. Schlosser.
For S. E. Schlosser's original version of this tale, and other great folk stories,
please visit www.americanfolklore.net.

Thank you to all of the storytellers who keep American folklore alive.

LAS

To my Babe.

PN

Do you know any tall tales?
What is a tall tale, you ask?

A tall tale is a story that is grand.
When a tall tale is told, you think it cannot be true,
but the story is told as if it is a true fact.

This is one of the many tall tales about
the woodcutter Paul Bunyan.

Paul Bunyan was said to be the biggest lumberjack ever to swing an ax. He stood as tall as a redwood tree. The footprints Paul left were as big as lakes!

Paul's pal and sidekick was his blue ox named Babe.
Babe was big, too. She was bigger than a caboose!

One winter, Paul Bunyan and Babe settled
a logging camp on the banks of a river.

You can bet that a big man like Paul could get
very hungry, so the kitchen in Paul Bunyan's
logging camp was about ten miles long!

Paul's big kitchen had a huge stove in it.
This stove was as tall as a pine tree.

When Paul's stove was filled with firewood
and it got hot, it felt like summer
in the logging camp when it was winter!

One day, at about noontime,
Paul Bunyan told his camp cook
that he felt like pancakes for lunch.
"I'm in the mood for some flapjacks,"
he said.

So the camp cook set off to make flapjacks.

First of all, the flapjack griddle was as big as a ballroom! The griddle was put on the big stove, then men swooshed across it on sleds made of bacon. This would keep the flapjacks from sticking to the griddle as they cooked.

Next, the cook mixed the batter in a dish as big as a swimming pool.

Five men dumped buckets of batter onto the hot griddle.

The batter oozed
and sizzled.

As the flapjacks
cooked, it took
five more men
just to flip them!

Soon, there was a ten-foot-tall stack of flapjacks next to Paul Bunyan. But this stack did not fill Paul up. The cook needed to make some more!

All of the rest of the woodsmen in the logging camp had to sit on the kitchen's ten-mile-long table until Paul Bunyan had his fill of flapjacks.

As the woodsmen sat and sat, Paul's pal Babe got restless. So restless, in fact, that she kicked a bag of peas off of the kitchen table.

The peas went far when Babe kicked them. They went out of the kitchen, and many of them landed in a hot spring.

18

Well, that hot spring got the peas cooking
and the camp cook added some salt and bacon.

And then do you know what happened?

All of the woodsmen and Paul Bunyan got to have
hot peas and broth for lunch for the rest of the winter.

That is, when Paul Bunyan didn't ask
the camp cook for more pancakes for lunch!

## Prerequisite Skills

Single consonants and short vowels
Final double consonants **ff, gg, ll, nn, ss, tt, zz**
Consonant /k/ **ck**
Consonant /j/ **g, dge**
Consonant /s/ **c**
Consonant digraphs /ng/ **ng, n[k]**, /th/ **th**, /hw/ **wh**
Consonant digraphs /ch/ **ch, tch**, /sh/ **sh**, /f/ **ph**
Schwa /ə/ **a, e, i, o, u**
Long /ā/ **a_e**
Long /ē/ **e_e, ee, y**
Long /ī/ **i_e, igh**
Long /ō/ **o_e**
Long /ū/, /ōo/ **u_e**
**r**-Controlled /ar/ **ar**
**r**-Controlled /or/ **or**
**r**-Controlled /ûr/ **er, ir, ur, ear, or, [w]or**
Variant vowel /aw/ **al, all**
Consonant /l/ **le**
/d/ or /t/ **–ed**

**Prerequisite Skills** are foundational phonics skills that have been previously introduced.

**Target Letter-Sound Correspondence** is the letter-sound correspondence introduced in the story.

**High-Frequency Puzzle Words** are high-frequency irregular words.

**Story Puzzle Words** are irregular words that are not high frequency.

**Decodable Words** are words that can be decoded solely on the basis of the letter-sound correspondences or phonetic elements that have been introduced.

## Target Letter-Sound Correspondence

Short /oo/ sound spelled **oo**

| | |
|---|---|
| cook | redwood |
| cooked | stood |
| cooking | took |
| firewood | woodcutter |
| foot | woodsmen |
| footprints | |

## Target Letter-Sound Correspondence

Long /ōo/ sound spelled **oo**

| | |
|---|---|
| ballroom | pool |
| caboose | soon |
| mood | swooshed |
| noontime | too |
| oozed | |

## Story Puzzle Words

| | |
|---|---|
| blue | peas |
| Paul | true |
| Paul's | told |

## High-Frequency Puzzle Words

| | |
|---|---|
| about | put |
| any | said |
| be | she |
| could | so |
| day | some |
| do | there |
| from | they |
| have | to |
| he | was |
| know | were |
| many | what |
| of | would |
| one | you |
| out | |

# Decodable Words

| | | | | | |
|---|---|---|---|---|---|
| a | Bunyan's | got | left | pancakes | tale |
| across | but | grand | like | pine | tales |
| added | camp | griddle | logging | rest | tall |
| all | can | had | long | restless | ten |
| an | cannot | happened | lumberjack | river | than |
| and | did | help | lunch | salt | that |
| as | didn't | his | made | sat | the |
| ask | dish | hot | make | set | them |
| at | dumped | huge | man | settled | then |
| ax | ever | hungry | men | sidekick | think |
| Babe | fact | I'm | mile | sit | this |
| bacon | far | if | miles | sizzled | tree |
| bag | felt | in | mixed | sleds | until |
| banks | fill | is | more | spring | up |
| batter | filled | it | named | stack | very |
| bet | first | just | needed | sticky | well |
| big | five | keep | next | story | went |
| bigger | flapjack | kicked | not | stove | when |
| biggest | flapjacks | kitchen | off | summer | winter |
| broth | flip | kitchen's | on | swimming | with |
| buckets | for | lakes | ox | swing | |
| Bunyan | get | landed | pal | table | |